megabat

Daniel hates the sound of camp. Leeches, outhouses, bad food, new people . . . bugs!

Megabat loves the sound of camp! Little cabins, buttermelon, new friends, pranks . . . bugs!

Daniel makes friends on the first day, and he doesn't see a single leech in the lake. And he does like the campfire sing-alongs and scary stories.

Megabat makes a new friend too, a friend who wants him to explore the spooky woods and ominous-sounding caves. No thanking yours.

Daniel discovers camp isn't so bad. Friendship bracelets, puzzles and tie dying are more fun than he thought, and who doesn't love a waffle breakfast?

As Megabat tries to avoid a scary outing into the woods, he teaches his new friend crafts too, with increasingly disastrous results. And he can't even eat waffles!

Will Megabat find enough courage to go flying in the forest? Will Daniel learn to love Camp Wildwood? And what will happen when the camp counselors find out there are bats living in Cabin 8? Camp really is the adventure of a livingtime!

Paperback edition published by Tundra Books, 2021

Text copyright © 2020 by Anna Humphrey
Illustrations copyright © 2020 by Kass Reich

Tundra Books, an imprint of Penguin Random House Canada Young Readers,
a division of Penguin Random House of Canada Limited

Library and Archives Canada Cataloguing in Publication

Title: Megabat is a fraidybat / Anna Humphrey ; illustrated by Kass Reich.
Names: Humphrey, Anna, author. | Reich, Kass, illustrator.
Series: Humphrey, Anna. Megabat (Series)
Description: Series statement: Megabat | Previously published: Toronto: Tundra Books, 2020.
Identifiers: Canadiana 20200181971 | ISBN 9780735268050 (softcover)
Classification: LCC PS8615.U457 M44 2021 | DDC jC813/.6—dc23

Published simultaneously in the United States of America by Tundra Books
of Northern New York, an imprint of Penguin Random House Canada Young Readers,
a division of Penguin Random House of Canada Limited

Library of Congress Control Number: 2019944755

Edited by Samantha Swenson
Designed by John Martz
The artwork in this book was rendered in graphite.
The text was set in Caslon 540 LT Std.

Printed and bound in the United States of America

www.penguinrandomhouse.ca

1 2 3 4 5   25 24 23 22 21

Penguin
Random House
tundra   TUNDRA BOOKS

ANNA HUMPHREY

illustrated by KASS REICH

MEGABAT

IS A **FRAIDYBAT**

tundra

For Grace and Elliot:
two of the bravest kids I know

1

A WILDWOOD WELCOME

It was the second week of summer vacation, and Daniel, who'd just flopped down on the grass in his backyard, groaned.

"Justing one more!" Megabat urged. The little fruit bat perched on his friend's forehead and leaned over to peer into his eyes. "Peeeeeze!"

"Oh, okay." Daniel gave in. "But this
is the *last* one."

They were playing Would You Rather?
It was a game the friends normally used
for long, dull waits . . . like when Daniel's
parents stood in line at the bank. You
had to say two choices, then each player

decided which one was best . . . or least-bad.

"It's being Birdgirl's turn." Megabat gazed at his beloved—a pretty-pretty pigeon who shared the backyard shed with him.

She scratched thoughtfully at the ground with one foot, like she was trying to come up with a good one, then bobbed her head when she had it. She pecked at something in the grass. "Coo-woo?" She pecked at something else. "Ooo coo-woo?"

Megabat translated. "Hers is saying, 'Would yours rather snack on this tiny rock *or* this dryish bit of grass?'"

"Seriously?" Daniel rolled his eyes.

"That's the same question she asked last time!"

"Nonetrue! Last time hers ask-ded if yours would rather snack on a bit of poppy-corn floating in a puddle or swallowings a lump of dirt."

Daniel sighed. "Well, all her questions are about eating stuff off the ground."

It was true. Ground-food was Birdgirl's favorite.

"This is getting kind of boring." Daniel yawned.

Even Megabat couldn't really disagree. The friends had been looking forward to summer holidays for ages, but it had only taken a few days for them to finish everything on the "Big List of Such-Fun

Stuff to Do" that they'd made during the last week of school.

They'd started by re-watching all the Star Wars movies—twice—then moved on to drinking strawberry Jell-O through a straw; taking fashion photos of Priscilla, Daniel's purebred cat; seeing how many letters of the alphabet they could burp before they ran out of breath; and finding out how refreshing it would be if they filled water balloons with lemonade. ("More stickier than roofreshing," Megabat had concluded.)

Talia, their friend who lived next door, was at horseback riding camp all day, and now they were even bored of playing the game they played when they were bored.

Things were looking glum.

Megabat sighed heavily, then began to make a pop-pop-pop sound with his lips. He'd taught himself this noise the week before. It made a satisfying smack and helped to pass the time.

"Would you stop that?" Daniel said after a minute, clearly annoyed.

"Oka-hay, fine!" Megabat rolled off Daniel's forehead into the grass. "Perhapsing ours could read Diamond Foot," the bat suggested. Diamond Foot was the world's most valuable graphic novel superhero—and not just because his right foot was made of a flawless one-thousand-carat diamond. He wore a cool costume, stomped out bad guys

wherever he found them and put his foot down firmly in the face of injustice.

He even had his own catchphrase: "A brilliant hero has zero fear-o!" Oh, the action! The adventure! The twinkly-twinkly toes! Megabat loved reading that book with Daniel.

"It's a great story," Daniel said, "but we've already read it. Sixteen hundred times. We should wait until the new one comes out at the end of the month."

"That's being zeons away!" Megabat whined.

Daniel didn't pay any attention. He was busy staring at the clouds. "I wish something exciting would happen," he said idly.

And, just then, something *did* happen—but whether it was exciting or terrible was a matter of opinion.

"There you are!" Daniel's dad came out the back door. "I've got a special delivery for you."

Quick as a flash, Megabat ducked under Daniel's baseball cap, which had been left lying on the grass. He always had to stay out of sight when grown-ups were around. Some of them screamed or chased him with a broom.

Daniel's dad crossed the grass, and Megabat peered out from under the cap to see the delivery: a big flat yellow envelope with writing on it.

"A letter?" Daniel sat up. "For me?

I never get mail. Who's it from?"

Daniel's dad handed it over with a smile. "Open it and see."

Daniel ripped the envelope open and pulled out a glossy folder. Megabat had to crane his neck a little to see. It had pictures of pointy trees on the front.

"Welcome to Camp Wildwood," Daniel read. *"Camp Wildwood?"*

"Mom and I wanted to surprise you. So . . . surprise!" his father said. "It's your welcome package. You're going to sleepaway camp! At Camp Wildwood on the shores of beautiful Lake Pinecrest."

Megabat could see that Daniel's eyes had gone wide with panic.

"You know about Wildwood!" Daniel's

dad went on. "The camp I went to when I was your age."

"The one with the outhouses? And the giant spiders?" Daniel's lip trembled.

"Well, sure. There was the odd spider in the outhouses . . . but they've got indoor plumbing now. I met some of my best friends there. It's also where I did my first archery lesson. And where I learned to skip stones and do a loon call."

Daniel's father cupped his hands around his mouth and flapped his fingers. It made an echoey whistle that rose and fell, rose and fell. The sound reminded Megabat of the bright-beaked birds in the jungles of Borneo where he'd been born.

"And remember the funny story about the underpants and the flagpole?" Daniel's father smiled fondly.

Megabat thought that sounded like a great story.

Daniel crossed his arms over his chest. "I don't want to go."

"How do you know? You haven't tried it yet," his father said reasonably.

"I won't know anyone. And there'll be bugs!"

Bugs! Megabat began to make a list in his head of his favorites. Ladybugs were a cheerful reddish color. Potato bugs curled into little balls when you poked them, and he loved the *sproing* of a good grasshopper. What other bugs might be at camp, he wondered.

"That's what bug spray's for," Daniel's dad said. "And you'll make friends before you know it. You'll see," he promised. "Sleepaway camp is the adventure of a lifetime."

"I HATE adventures!" Daniel yelled.

"Just take a look, okay?" Daniel's dad pointed to the folder. "We'll talk about it more later."

As soon as Daniel's dad went inside, Megabat climbed out from under the hat and came to perch on his friend's shoulder. "Opening it!" he urged.

The first sheet had pictures of boats, marshmallows on sticks, and kids painting birdhouses. It said "Activities and Crafts." Underneath was a paper marked "Your Cabin." It showed two kids sitting on top of a double-decker bed. The last sheet said "Food." There was a grown-up lady in a tall white hat and children gathered at long tables. Megabat liked that one best of all. "Ooooooh!" He drooled over a photo of a girl eating a big slice of melon.

Suddenly, Daniel threw the folder onto the grass and began to cry.

Megabat peered at his friend curiously for a moment, then he used his long tongue to lick away the tears. "Why is yours mad and sad?" he asked gently.

"I'm not mad and sad." Daniel said,

wrapping his arms around his knees. "I'm scared."

"For why?"

"For camp. It's going to be awful."

Megabat didn't understand. "But camp is being the adventure of a livingtime!"

Daniel wiped his cheeks with the back of his hand, leaving dirty smudges. "That's just what parents say to trick you into going. I've seen camp on TV and read about it in books. I'll have to sleep in a leaky old cabin. They'll feed me gray slop for breakfast, lunch and dinner. And, worst of all, I'll be all alone." Daniel dissolved into shuddery sobs.

"No yours won't." Megabat spread his

wings wide. "Because Megabat will alsowise be adventuring to Camp Wildwood on the shores of Lake PieCrust!"

"You will?"

"Undoubtedly!"

Megabat went almost everywhere with Daniel. Plus, surely the camp Daniel knew from TV and books was a different one altogether. As far as Megabat could tell, it sounded nothing like the pictures in the folder or the place Daniel's father had described.

"Making craftses! Riding boatses! Catching bugses! Ours will be having *such much* fun," the little bat promised. "Yours will see." He licked one last tear,

then put his wingtips on his hips and
stuck out his chest in a super-pose, just
like Diamond Foot. "Nonething is
fearsome when Megabat's nearsome!"

2

THE BIG YELLOW BUS

Even though Megabat kept reminding Daniel that camp would be fun, when leaving day came, Daniel was still scared.

"Birdgirl and I made you guys a care package." Talia from next door had come over to say goodbye.

"Miew!" Priscilla the cat wound around Talia's ankles and glared up at her indignantly.

"And Priscilla helped by suggesting that we add the sparkly bow," Talia added. She leaned down to scratch the cat's ears before handing Daniel a box with a big, glittery ribbon on top. "It's got puzzle books, candy, juice boxes, glow-in-the-dark eyeball stickers and stamps so you can write letters to us if you have time."

"Coo-woo," cried Birdgirl. The pigeon was perched on a tree branch near the front door. "Coo-woooooo."

"Mine will missing yours alsowise, Birdgirl. But ours will be home in justing one week with new friends and adventuresome stories to tell." Megabat repeated the things Daniel's parents kept saying. "Rights, Daniel?"

"Maybe." Daniel sighed. "If we don't drown in the leech-infested lake or get poisoned by the food first."

"Okay." Daniel's mother closed the trunk of the car. "Time to go, sweetie."

Megabat gave Birdgirl a peck on the cheek, Daniel pet the cat and waved miserably to Talia, and the friends got into the backseat. While they drove, Daniel's parents talked about the greatness and fun-ness of camp. Megabat—hidden inside the cup holder—listened, getting more and more excited, but Daniel just stared out the window. Finally, they pulled into a big lot. It was empty except for a few cars and a bunch of families standing around with luggage.

"This must be the spot!" Daniel's mother popped the trunk and got out.

Megabat frowned. It didn't look like the pictures. Where were the little log cabins and sailboats? There was a large puddle where the pavement dipped. Could that be beautiful Lake PieCrust?

"Don't worry," Daniel said, noticing Megabat's confusion. "This isn't camp."

Megabat followed Daniel's gaze. Turning into the parking lot was a big yellow bus!

Megabat couldn't contain his excitement. "Ours is riddening a school bus to camp?!"

"Yup," Daniel said miserably. "It's going to take us a million miles from civilization."

After many hugs, a few photos and some fresh tears, it was time to board. With Megabat tucked into his pocket, Daniel joined a lineup of laughing, jostling children.

When it was their turn to climb the stairs, the bus driver gave Daniel a big smile. "First time at camp?" he asked.

Daniel, whose eyes were still red from crying, nodded.

"Tell you what," the driver said. "A week from now, I'll be bringing you home. If you can tell me ten things you

did that were fun, I'll give you this
bobblehead."

Megabat peered out to see a figurine
on the dashboard. It was an Ewok—a
character from Star Wars that looks like a

teddy bear. When the bus driver touched its head, it danced in a delightful wibbly-wobbly way. Megabat had never wanted anything so badly before!

"Sure," Daniel muttered. "But I can tell you right now, you'll end up keeping it."

"We'll see about that." The driver winked, then turned to salute the next kid getting on the bus.

Daniel walked down the aisle, past the rows of tall, dark-green benches. He picked one and sank down. As the other kids filed on, they took the seats around him, but nobody sat next to Daniel—which was just as well because Megabat was much too excited to stay quiet.

"Mine has longly dreamed of riddening a school bus." He hung over the edge of Daniel's pocket to see out the window. "Is ours leaving yet?"

"Shhhh. Not yet, Megabat. You'll feel it when the bus starts, okay?"

"All aboard!" the driver called merrily. "Next stop, Camp Wildwood!"

Like a sleeping dragon, the bus roared to life.

"Wahoooo!" Megabat cried in glee.

The bus lurched forward, then backed up and lurched again. Daniel clutched his stomach. "I think I'm gonna puke."

Meanwhile, Megabat was having the time of his life. "Wheeeeeeeee!" he shouted as he flailed back and forth.

"Huh?" A boy with dark, curly hair turned around in the seat in front of them. Daniel only just managed to push Megabat's head down into the pocket in time. "Did you say something?"

"Oh . . . um . . . ," Daniel answered nervously. "Not really."

The bus pulled out of the lot, turning sharply and sending the kids sliding on their green benches.

"Oh," the boy said. "I thought you were yelling wheeeeee!" He shrugged and turned back in his seat, but a moment later the bus took another sudden turn.

"Wahooooo! Ours is out of controooool!"

The curly-haired boy turned again. He pointed to Daniel's shirt pocket. "Okay, maybe *you* didn't say anything. But your talking bat sure loves school buses."

3

IRWIN APPLEMAN

The boy's name was Irwin.

"Irwin Appleman." He held out a
hand.

"Daniel," Daniel answered, shaking
it uncertainly.

Irwin checked to make sure the driver
wasn't watching, then he grabbed his
backpack, swung around and slid into
the seat beside Daniel. "Don't worry,"

Irwin whispered. "I won't tell anyone there's a bat on the bus, *or* that it can talk. Some kids would freak out. Like Devan Baker. Last summer a butterfly landed on him and he nearly fainted."

Megabat liked Irwin Appleman—and not just because his name sounded like a fruit. He had a confident, no-nonsense way about him that made him seem trustworthy.

"And what's your name, little guy?" Irwin held out the tip of a pinky finger for Megabat to shake, which Megabat did, feeling very important indeed.

"Mine's Megabat," the bat said, with a little bow. "Nicely to meet yours."

"It's—um—nicely to meet yours too."

Irwin flashed a silvery smile.

"Ooooooh!" Megabat was dazzled. He motioned with one wing for Irwin to sink lower in the seat, then climbed up Irwin's shirt collar to get a better look.

"What sparkly tooth decorations yours gots."

"You like my braces?" Irwin opened wider so Megabat could touch the small, metal squares.

"Yours is like Diamond Foot!" Megabat remarked. "Only with yours's face!"

"You read Diamond Foot too? That's my favorite graphic novel series. Actually . . ." He dug around in his backpack. "I just got this."

Daniel gasped. "No way!"

The cover of the book showed Diamond Foot battling a five-headed lizard while kicking his way through a brick building to rescue a screaming lady.

"That's being the dumbbell in distress." Megabat pointed to the lady. He felt clever for knowing the special words that meant "person who needs rescuing."

"He means *damsel* in distress," Daniel corrected. He looked at the book with awe. "This doesn't come out for two more weeks though!"

Irwin winked. "My mom's a librarian, so I've got connections. You can read it if you want."

"Seriously?" Daniel's eyes had gone wide.

"Of course!" Irwin said. "Be my guests."

Daniel used careful fingers to open

the cover, and then all three of them leaned over, reading together. The story began with a strange rumbling noise coming from the ground in Carbon City, where Diamond Foot lived and fought crime. As a purple mist drifted out of a sewer, one of the lizard's fearsome heads emerged.

The boys and the bat got so busy reading that they barely noticed the bus bump-bumping along. In fact, they didn't even look up until they got to the panel where a skunk passed out because the lizard's breath smelled so bad. Irwin and Daniel both laughed.

"Aha!" Megabat pointed with his wingtip. "Mine sees fun!"

"What?" Daniel asked, still laughing.

"Daniel is having *one* fun! Ours only needses nine mores."

Then, because Irwin didn't know yet, Megabat explained how Daniel was afraid to go to camp, and how the driver had promised them the Ewok bobblehead if he had ten kinds of fun.

"Don't worry," Irwin said. "You'll easily have more than that. This is my third year at Wildwood. It's the best."

The bus turned down a gravel road so narrow that tree branches brushed the windows on either side. Irwin closed the book. "Anyway, you'll see for yourself soon. We're here!"

Megabat peered out the window as

the bus emerged from the trees and
rolled to a stop.

Twelve red-roofed cabins stood in a
semicircle surrounded by towering pines.
There were larger buildings too, and a
fun-looking ropes course, and beyond all
that lay a glistening lake.

"Daniel!" Megabat turned. "Is yours
seeing this?"

But instead of admiring the beautiful
spot, Daniel was slapping at a tiny ant
that had crawled up his arm. He
scratched the spot where it had been and
blinked hard, like he might start crying
all over again.

4

FRUIT POPS AND
OTHER FUNS

As soon as the kids got off the bus, they were sorted into cabins. Daniel and Irwin were in Cabin 8, along with two boys who looked like copies of each other—except that one had long hair and one had short hair.

"These are the twins," Irwin said. "Gus and Rusty."

They also met their counselor—a tall, skinny man with a hairy face. "I'm Vijay." He extended a hand. From inside Daniel's pocket, Megabat watched as his friend reached out to shake it, then jumped back a second later—still holding the hand!

"AHHH!" Megabat shouted. Luckily, Vijay was too busy laughing to hear him.

"What the—?" Daniel dropped it.

"The old plastic-hand gag." Vijay wiped a tear from his eye. "New campers fall for it every time." He poked his real hand out of his sleeve to show where it had been hiding all along, and Daniel smiled nervously.

"Vijay's famous for his pranks," Irwin

explained. "But don't worry. We'll get him back before the week's over. Anyway, come on!" Irwin took off across the field at a run. "I want to get a top bunk."

It was dark inside Cabin 8, but as soon as Megabat's eyes adjusted to the dimness, he saw that it was cozy too. There were four beds—two top ones and two bottom ones—a bathroom and a separate room that said Counselor's Quarters on the door.

"I think we should choose a lower bunk," Daniel said to Megabat as he set their things down. "That way the roof won't leak on us when it rains at night."

"Hmmmmm." The bat leaned back

in Daniel's pocket, trying to get a better look at the ceiling. The top bunks seemed more fun. They had ladders and a little nook for storing things. Maybe they could have one if Megabat could reassure Daniel that there weren't any holes in the roof.

"Lets mine inspect for leakies." He flapped up to the bunk above.

"I call top bunk!"

Unfortunately, the twins picked that moment to arrive. Gus—the long-haired boy—launched his overflowing duffel bag up onto the mattress. Megabat barely managed to flap out of the way in time to avoid getting crushed.

"Hey! Watching where yours chucks

stuffs!" he yelled indignantly.

"Huh?" Gus stopped in his tracks. "Who said that? Was it you?" he asked Daniel. Daniel shook his head, and the boy climbed the ladder to look around. Megabat edged into a dark corner.

"Irwin?" the boy asked. "Did you say that?" But he didn't wait for an answer. "Oh, I get it! It's one of Vijay's practical jokes. Good one, Vijay," he called loudly. "Where are you hiding?"

"Uh . . ." The short-haired twin was standing in the doorway holding his bags and a butterfly net he'd brought from home. "Vijay's still at the bus welcoming campers with his fake hand," he said. "I can see him from here."

"He must have left a recorder then."
Gus started ripping the sheets off his
bed. "It's gotta be here somewhere."

Irwin sighed. "We should probably
just tell them," he said to Daniel.

"Tell us what?" Rusty asked.

"That Daniel brought his talking fruit
bat to camp," Irwin answered.

Rusty laughed. "Yeah. Right."

"Nice try, Irwin," Gus added. "But
we're not dumb."

"It's true. There's a bat up there. And
he can talk!"

Megabat couldn't help but take
offense. "A-hem! Excusing mine!" He
flapped out of the corner and came to
perch on the edge of the bunk.

The twins jumped back.

"Mine can do *mores* than talking! Megabat is alsowise a splendiferous dancer." He tap-tapped his feet to show them. "And mine can do headstandings!" He demonstrated that as well, nearly falling off the bunk. "*And* make a pop-pop-pop noise for an extremely longish time!" He popped his lips to make his fun noise.

"Megabat!" Daniel warned. "Please don't start that again. You'll drive everyone crazy."

"Oooookay, then. That's a talking, dancing, popping bat," Rusty admitted. His brother Gus didn't seem ready to believe it though.

"Are you sure it's real?" He poked
Megabat in the tummy. Megabat poked
him back in the forehead. "Yup, it's real,"
Gus conceded.

"Don't tell anyone else, okay?" Daniel
pleaded.

"You have to promise!" Irwin urged.

"None of the other kids can know he's part of our cabin. And we *especially* can't let Vijay see him."

"Let me see who?" They all turned to find their counselor standing in the doorway. He was looking down at a clipboard, which gave Megabat just enough time to hide behind Gus's duffel bag.

"Uhhhhhh . . . my bear." Daniel reached into his bag and pulled out Teddy—the old brown bear he slept with. He sounded a little embarrassed to be showing it in front of the other boys. "I—um—don't want you to tease me or do any pranks with it."

"Not to worry," Vijay reassured him.

"Bears are cool. And they're strictly off limits for pranks. Now, guys, bathing suits on! The first cabin with all its campers in the lake gets free treats from the Tuck Shop. Do we want to win, or do we want to WIN?"

The other boys rushed to change, but not Daniel. He put on his bathing suit slowly, muttering about bloodsucking leeches. Irwin had to drag him out by the arm (with Megabat wrapped up in a towel), and even then, while Irwin did a huge cannonball off the end of the dock, and the twins splashed in up to their necks, Daniel only got his toes wet.

"It still counts!" Irwin said, treading water. "We win!"

Kids from other cabins groaned, but there was lots of splashing around from Cabin 8. Even Daniel joined in when the other boys cheered, "Cabin 8 is super-great!" Plus, he seemed to relax when, after they got out of the water, he and Megabat found a quiet spot on the beach to check his feet.

"None leeches!" Megabat reported.

Next, it was dinner. There was spaghetti, garlic bread and a salad bar—but no fruit. "What about this?" Daniel slipped a slice of tomato to Megabat, who was hiding underneath his napkin, but Megabat wrinkled his nose.

"Scientifically speaking, a tomato is a fruit because it has seeds," Rusty explained. He seemed to know a lot about nature. All the same, Megabat turned up his nose. "Mine's not snacky," he said, although his tummy rumbled.

"Suit yourself," Daniel answered between bites of garlic bread. "I'm starving. I was expecting gray slop. But this food is actually pretty good!"

"Wait'll you try Cook Martina's award-winning waffles tomorrow morning," Gus answered.

After dinner there was free time. Some kids went swimming. Others hiked the trails. But the boys from Cabin 8 made straight for the Tuck Shop to get Popsicles and ice cream.

They were all sitting under a shady

tree, Daniel and Megabat sharing licks of a delicious fruit pop, when Daniel leapt up and started shaking his arm.

"Something's crawling on me!" he shouted. "Get it off!" Megabat, who'd been hanging out of Daniel's pocket, flapped away in alarm.

"Relax." Irwin got to his feet. "It's just a bug." He removed it with one finger.

Rusty leaned over. "Actually, it's a marmorated stinkbug. You can tell by the bands on its antennae. They're pretty rare around these parts."

Except for a few flies, this was the first bug Megabat had seen since getting to camp. "Oooooh!" he landed on Irwin's shoulder to get a better look. "Can mine keeping it for mine bug collection?" he asked.

"You don't have a bug collection," Daniel pointed out.

"He does now!" Rusty licked the last bits of ice cream from his container, then lifted the bug off Irwin's hand and put it inside. "Just be careful not to scare it," he warned. "Stinkbugs fart in self-defense."

Even Daniel thought that was cool. He came closer to look at the beetle and helped pick some leaves for it to munch on. Megabat named his stink beetle Whiffy. And that reminded Gus and the other boys of some rude jokes they knew. Soon everyone was laughing.

"Hey, Daniel," Gus said, catching his breath after an especially gross one. "Know any?"

"Nah." Daniel looked down at his shoes and, for a moment, Megabat felt sad for his friend. "I mean, I could *try* to tell a fart joke . . . but it would probably stink."

All of Cabin 8 burst out laughing, but Megabat laughed hardest—not just because Daniel's joke was funny but because he was relieved to see his friend having fun.

Later, as the other boys walked ahead to get ready for the campfire, Daniel scritched Megabat's ears. "Thanks," he said.

"For whats?" Megabat asked.

"You kept telling me camp wouldn't be scary. And you were right. Actually, I kind of like it here. Even the bugs are pretty neat." Daniel held up the stinkbug's ice-cream-container habitat. "There are no leeches . . . and I haven't been bitten by a single mosquito yet!"

"Ha! Mine told yours!"

Megabat grinned, then he sighed. The moon was peeking out from between the pines. The stars were twinkling. It was a perfect evening and—what's more— Megabat had counted at least three more funs to tell the bus driver about: fruit pops, new friends and fart jokes. Megabat had never been more content.

But that was *before* he heard the ghost story.

5

THE GHOST STORY

"This happened a long time ago," a counselor began. Flickering flames lit up her face as she leaned forward. "At this very camp."

The boys and girls were huddled together on logs around a campfire. They'd already sung songs and roasted marshmallows. And now Fiona, the counselor from Cabin 3, was trying to frighten them before bedtime.

It wasn't going to work—at least not on Megabat—who was relaxing inside Irwin's upside-down baseball cap. "Mine's not ascared," he muttered. After all, there'd been nothing scary so far. They'd just sung a song about a bunny named FouFou and done an equally silly chant about frogs on a log.

"It was a clear night, like this one." Fiona's long black hair swung back and forth as she glanced around at the trees, like she was expecting something to jump out. "Cook Martina was walking through the woods. She'd been out hiking, and she was on her way back to the kitchen to clean up after a big spaghetti dinner."

"Daniel," Megabat whispered, poking his friend's thigh. "Ours had passgetti tonight!" Megabat liked stories that reminded him of himself.

Daniel leaned down. "Shhhh," he whispered. "I know."

Fiona went on: "Everyone else was at the fire pit—which was exactly why Cook was surprised when—*crack, crack, crack*—she heard the noise of twigs snapping. It sounded like someone was coming through the woods behind her. 'Who's there?' she said, but nobody answered. She quickened her steps. *Woooooo. Woooooo.* There was another noise. Was it just the wind, rustling through the tall pines? She couldn't be sure, so Cook broke into a run.

"Soon, she reached the safety of the mess hall. She slammed the door behind her and went into the kitchen with a sigh of relief . . . but not a moment later . . . CREEEEEEAK—"

Two girls from Cabin 6 clutched each other's hands.

"From inside the kitchen, Cook heard the mess hall door open. Then, *clomp, clomp, clomp* . . . footsteps crossed the floor."

Megabat scoffed. "Squeakish doors and stepping feets aren't ascary," he muttered to himself.

The counselor went on, "Cook told herself it was no big deal. Probably just a camper coming in for a snack. She turned on the tap to wash some dishes, but suddenly . . ." The counselor sat up taller and made wispy shapes with her hands. "She heard a ghostly voice just behind her."

"What did it say?" a girl with braids asked.

"It said . . . 'I am the ghoooooost of the past. Aaaaaaaaahhhhh.'" Fiona almost whispered the words.

Megabat hunched his wings up. He still wasn't afraid, but he didn't like this story quite as much anymore.

"Cook whirled on the spot. *BANG*

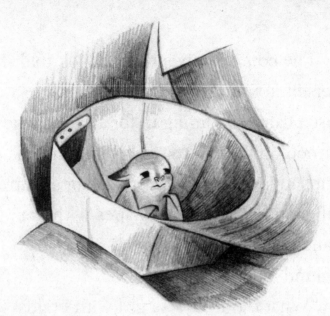

BANG BANG!" the counselor shouted.
"All around her pots and pans started
rattling, and the voice came again:
'I AM THE GHOST OF THE PAST.
AHHHHHHH!'"

"Daniel," Megabat whispered. He
didn't want to hear anymore. He was
ready to go back to the cabin.

"Shhh, Megabat," Daniel said, "I want to find out how it ends."

"'Wh-wh-what do you want, ghost of the past?' Cook said. 'I'll give you anything!' But the voice only answered, 'I AM THE GHOST OF THE PAST. AHHHHHHH! I AM THE GHOST OF THE PAST. AHHHHHHH!'"

Fiona leapt to her feet, making almost everyone scream. Suddenly, her voice switched from scary to friendly. "'I am the ghost of the pasta. Can I please have some leftover spaghetti with tomato sauce and Parmesan cheese?'"

Some of the kids laughed right away. Others took a little longer to get it.

"The ghost of the *past, ahhhhh. The*

ghost of the pasta. Get it?" Irwin explained to Gus, who was still looking puzzled.

A boy from Cabin 5 groaned. "Tell us the truth!" he said. "You just made that up, didn't you?"

"And it's your corniest campfire story yet," Irwin added.

The counselor gave a little bow. "*Did* I make it up though?" she said. "Can you be certain?" Then she pointed to the pathway. "Okay, back to the cabins to bed, guys!"

The kids lit flashlights and made their way through the shadowy woods.

"She had me going for a while there," Gus admitted, while the boys were all putting on their pajamas.

"Not me," Irwin said.

"Me neither," Daniel said. "Not at all."

"Sheesh! Ghost of the pasta!" Megabat scoffed in agreement. He hung himself upside down from one of the slats above Daniel's bunk to settle in for a sleep. "Much unscary," he added, as he tried to hide the little shiver that ran down the back of his wings.

"All right." Vijay popped his head in from his counselor's room. "Lights out." He flicked a switch and the cabin went dark.

Megabat tried to drift off, but the bunk slats felt different from his usual roosting spot in the shed at home. He wasn't sure he'd be able to sleep without

Birdgirl's comforting, cooing snores. And he couldn't stop thinking about the pasta ghost.

"Daniel!" Megabat whispered into the darkness.

"Yeah."

"Mines not sleepy."

"Try counting sheep," Daniel suggested.

It was dark in the cabin, but the porch light was on, so he could see well enough to count. "None," Megabat reported. "There's being none sheep."

"No, I mean, imagine sheep in your head, then count them."

Megabat didn't see how *that* was going to help.

"Daniel!" he whispered again.

"What, Megabat?" Daniel sounded a little impatient.

"Let's playing Would Yours Rather. Mine will going first! Would yours rather . . . hmmmmm . . . never watching Star Wars movies again or never eating buttermelon for the resting of yours's life?"

To Megabat, it was an impossible question, but Rusty knew his answer right away. "Easy," he chimed in from the other side of the room. "Give up buttermelon, whatever that is."

"He means *water*melon," Daniel explained.

"Still," Irwin agreed, "I'd take

Wookiees over watermelon any day."

After that, everyone had turns asking questions, and Megabat learned a lot about their new friends. For example, Gus would rather have a monkey's face than a pig's nose. Irwin would rather be a tiny elephant than a giant mouse, and everyone agreed they'd rather cry chocolate syrup than sneeze caramel sauce.

Irwin was the first to yawn.

"Sorry, guys," he whispered. "I'm falling asleep."

"I'm beat too," Gus agreed.

"Good night, Daniel."

"Night, Irwin."

"Night, Gus and Rusty."

"Good night, Megabat."

"Goodly sleepings," Megabat answered—but he didn't fall asleep. In fact, he *couldn't* fall asleep. Now that there was no one to keep him company, his big ears were wide open, and there were many strange noises coming from outside. Rustling. Buzzing. The hoot of an owl and then—*crack, crack, crack.*

This sound was closer than the others. Maybe even right outside the door!

Crack, crack, crack.

"Daniel!" Megabat poked his friend in the forehead.

Daniel groaned and rolled over. "Go to sleep, Megabat."

The little bat tried rocking himself

back and forth. He even imagined a few
sheep, but it was no use.

Crack, crack, crack.

Megabat thought the ghost of the
pasta was made-up. But that sound . . .
it was so eerie, and exactly like the

snapping of twigs that had come at the start of Fiona's story! Was something coming out of the deep, dark woods toward them?

Then Megabat had a horrible thought: "Mine's stinkbug!" The boys hadn't wanted him to bring Whiffy inside. The bug was on the porch in his habitat, all alone. What if he was frightened too?

"Nonething is fearsome when Megabat's nearsome," Megabat muttered to himself. Then he tried to say it with more conviction: "Nonething is fearsome when Megabat's nearsome." His tiny heart was pounding. His little knees were knocking. Still, Whiffy was counting on him! He pushed the door open and stepped onto the porch.

Crack, crack, crack.

Megabat whirled on the spot.

"Whiffy? Is that yours?" He squinted into the darkness. But there was nothing unusual . . . just a few pairs of rain boots and Rusty's butterfly net lying on the cabin's porch.

Crack, crack, crack.

His eyes followed the sound. Aha! Something was caught in the bottom of the net. It was banging around, trying to get free. Each time it struggled, the metal hoop of the net cracked against the wooden porch.

"Who-who-whose is there?" Megabat asked.

Tut-tut-tut. Eeeeek.

The sound that answered was part click, part squeal. A large beetle, perhaps? A mouse?

The creature shifted, then hissed, revealing sharp white fangs.

A wild bat!

6

THE WILD BATS

Megabat had seen other bats before.
When he lived on a papaya farm in
Borneo, he'd had a whole family with
brothers and sisters. But this bat looked
different. For one thing, she was even
smaller than him. For another, her fur
was brown where his was gray. And while
he had large, saucer-like ears, hers were

short and black. She was also extremely cranky.

She hissed again, baring her fangs, but Megabat knew she couldn't hurt him.

"Greetings, tiny bat," he said. "Mine can see yours is stuck in that's flutterby net."

The smaller bat narrowed her eyes and tried to inch backward.

"Mine won't hurting yours," he reassured her. "For fact, mine will be rescuing yours this night. Seeing?" He pointed at the net, which was tangled around her wings. "Yours is a dumbbell in distress."

The little bat didn't seem to like that. She hissed even louder than before.

"No, no! Yours is disunderstanding," Megabat explained. "Dumbbell in distress is not meaning yours is dumb. Its is meaning yours is in need of rescuing by a hero suchly as mine." He puffed his chest.

The little brown bat grimaced. But

there was no way around it; she really was stuck, which was probably why she let Megabat come closer.

"Hmmmm." He pulled the net this way and that. "Letting mine see. If mine loosenings this bit." He tugged at some of the slack. "And bite-ings this part in mine mouth." He took a few big steps back, tugging the string between his teeth. "And then mine just—uh-oh."

Megabat looked down. One of his feet was tangled in the net. "Well, if mine grabbings that off." He lay down on his back and curled himself into a ball to reach his foot but snagged one of his wingtips in the process.

The smaller bat shot Megabat a

withering look, as if to say, *"Who's the dumbbell now?"* Finally, she shook her head in dismay and gave a few short, sharp squeaks that sounded like laughter.

"Oka-hay," Megabat admitted. He always tried to be a good sport. "Hardy-har-har. Squeakety-squeak-squeak. Mine is alsowise stuck. Its is being joke-worthy. But whats will ours doing *now*?"

In answer, the smaller bat opened her mouth and began to sing. It was a high-pitched squealing song that carried out into the starry night. To tell the truth, it hurt Megabat's ears.

"Mine isn't meaning to be rude," he said, after a while, "but perhaps ours can make a fun pop-pop-pop sound together insteadly." He demonstrated. "Or singing another song. Does yours know the one about the Rabbit FouFou?"

But the brown bat didn't seem to like his popping sound, and she either didn't know the rabbit song or didn't want to sing it. She kept right on squealing. Finally, she stopped. Megabat was about to breathe a sigh of relief when she glanced upward. He followed her gaze and gasped.

A dark creature was swooping toward them like something from a nightmare. From wing to wing, it was almost five times Megabat's size, and when it passed in front of the porch light, it cast an enormous shadow.

"Th-th-that's is a bogglingly big bat!" Megabat stammered.

The big brown bat locked eyes on the little brown bat. With a terrific flapping it landed on the porch and, with one quick swipe of its razor-sharp claws, tore through the butterfly net and grabbed her in its powerful wings.

"Stop! Stop! Stopping it!" Megabat cried. "Mine demands yours stops smooshing hers!"

But then the big bat did a curious thing. It released the little bat ever-so-slightly and licked her head before pulling her close again.

"Oh. Oh! Mine sees!" Megabat said with relief as the big bat nuzzled the little bat's fur. "Yours are hugging. Because yours are a baby and mummy bat!"

Suddenly, big bat pushed her baby behind her. She approached Megabat with a series of sniffs, snarls and chirps. Megabat panicked: Did she think he was responsible for capturing her baby in the net? Was she about to suck his blood in revenge? Would Daniel wake up if Megabat cried for help?

Before Megabat could find out, the mother bat's sharp claws were coming toward him. He shut his eyes and made himself as small as possible inside the net.

There was a ripping, then more

chirps. Megabat opened his eyes and jumped back when he saw a large, wet nose in his face. The mother bat was smelling him. Meanwhile, the baby was saying something. Megabat didn't speak their chirpy language, but his blood hadn't been sucked, so he guessed she was explaining that he'd tried to help her.

Megabat gave a shaky little bow. "Greetings," he said. "Mine is Megabat." The two wild bats tilted their heads in confusion. "And yourses are being?" he prompted.

Megabat flashed them a smile when they still didn't answer. "That's being oka-hay. Mine didn't have a name until mine's Daniel gived mine one. Mine will calling yours . . ." He paused, scratching his head. "Babybat and Batzilla."

The mother bat opened her mouth and bared her fangs.

Megabat jumped back. "Or mine can calling yours something else if yours prefers."

The baby tilted her head to see her mother better, then she opened her mouth and showed her fangs too, but the corners of her mouth turned up a little more. Suddenly, Megabat saw what they were trying to do.

"Aha! Yours are learning to make smiles! Like suchly!" He gave them his brightest grin to demonstrate. They both came a little closer to examine his face, then tried again, but without as many teeth. "Muchly improved," Megabat said.

The mother bat pointed insistently at the floor of the porch with one wingtip.

"Yours wants mine to staying here?"

She nodded, then flew up to the roof of Cabin 8 and disappeared through an impossibly tiny crack. A moment later, she swooped back with something long and dangly in her talons. She dropped it at Megabat's feet.

"That's being a critterpillar."

Megabat had seen the long, fuzzy insects in Daniel's yard. They were always munching leaves. Batzilla nudged it closer. She wanted him to do something with it, but what?

"Mine could putting it in mine's bug habitat!" Megabat suggested. He went to get Whiffy's ice cream container, but when he dropped the wriggling caterpillar in beside the stinkbug, Babybat shrieked at him disapprovingly.

She picked out the caterpillar with one foot and mimed putting it into her mouth.

"Yours wants mine to eating it?" Megabat had to supress a shudder.

Babybat and Batzilla flashed him toothy smiles.

Now Megabat understood! They were never going to suck his blood. These were insect-eating bats, and they were giving him a treat.

"For thanking mine?" he guessed. "For yourses new names and for trying to help Babybat?"

They nodded.

Megabat approached the wriggler. He only liked eating fruits he knew.

Different foods were hard for him—even
when they didn't squirm. And yet,
Babybat and Batzilla were watching
him eagerly, like they couldn't wait to
see him enjoy his treat.

Megabat closed his eyes and held his
breath. He stuck out his long tongue and
touched the caterpillar with the very tip.

"Most scrumptious!" he proclaimed,
before turning his back and trying to
scrape the fuzzy feeling off his tongue.
The two bats seemed disappointed,
so Megabat went on. "For fact, so
scrumptious, mine must be saving it . . .
to sharing with mine's friend Daniel."

That seemed to satisfy them. The

mother motioned into the distance with her head.

"Yours must go hunting mores bugses now?" Megabat asked.

Batzilla pointed at Megabat, then into the deep, dark forest filled with strange sounds.

"And yours invites mine to come along?" Megabat asked.

Batzilla nodded.

Megabat gulped.

Babybat was eager to get going. She was already swooping around the porch light, eating moths and smacking her batty lips with glee.

He had to think fast. "Mine's tummy

will be filled with this scrumptious critterpillar." He faked a big yawn. "And mine is most nappy. Perhapsing tomorrow. Goodly night."

And then, because Batzilla was watching to make sure he got in safely, Megabat picked up the wiggling caterpillar and carried it with him.

7

FRAIDY-BAT

It was past midnight when Megabat
got to sleep, so he was groggy the next
morning when he awoke to Daniel
leaping out of bed.

"There's a bug on my pajamas!" He
was hopping around swatting at his leg
and shouting.

Finally, it was Irwin who climbed
down from his bunk to help. "It's just

a caterpillar." He lifted it off with his finger.

"Woopsy-doops. That's being mine's," Megabat said with a yawn and a stretch.

At first, Daniel was angry about the bug in his bed, but when Megabat explained about the wild bats he'd met the night before, all four boys gathered on the bed to listen.

"Theirs had pointy-pointy teeth," Megabat reported. "And the mummy bat was rhinormous."

"Were you scared?" Daniel asked.

"He wouldn't be scared of other bats." Irwin smiled, showing his magnificent braces. "Would you?"

"Of coursing not!" Megabat said.

Besides doing cannonballs off the dock, Irwin had already volunteered to go first for the ropes course that day. Megabat could never admit he'd been afraid to someone like Irwin. And he didn't want to tell Daniel he was scared either—not after he'd said so many times that there was nothing to be afraid of at camp!

"For fact," he went on, "mine did rescue Babybat." Megabat said it casually, like it was no big deal.

Irwin looked impressed by the rest of the story, but maybe that was because Megabat changed a few details here and there and left out the part where he got all tangled up and had to be rescued too.

And everyone agreed they'd rather do almost anything than eat a live caterpillar.

"So, I bet you're going flying with them tonight, right?" Irwin said. "Maybe explore some caves? If there are bats around, they probably gather at Devil's Mouth. The older campers go hiking there sometimes. People swear it's haunted—but that's probably not true."

Megabat didn't like strange, dark places . . . and he certainly didn't want to go anywhere that might be haunted, but he didn't want to sound like a fraidy-bat either.

"Ubsolutely!" Megabat boasted. "Ours will visit the deepest, darkest caves in all of Camp Wildwood tonight."

Thankfully, Megabat didn't have to think about that for much longer. Vijay told them to get dressed for waffles. Then, after breakfast, they were off to shoot arrows at the archery range, climb the ropes course, paddle canoes and tie-dye T-shirts.

The day passed in a blur, and before Megabat knew it, the sun was setting.

"I wonder what ghost story they'll tell tonight," Rusty said.

"Probably the ghost of the tune-ahhh," Daniel joked. "Because we had tuna casserole for dinner." The boys groaned. "You coming, Megabat?" He held out his hand, but the little bat shook his head. He hadn't liked the last ghost story, and he didn't want to hear another.

"He's going to explore the caves with the wild bats, remember?" Irwin said.

Megabat gulped, but he nodded.

As soon as the boys left, he settled in to read the rest of Irwin's Diamond Foot book. He hoped the wild bats would forget about him. But just as he reached the part where Diamond Foot kicks his way into a secret underground vault filled with rubies (nearly falling into the five-headed lizard's tricky trap), there was a knock at the window. Babybat's fang-filled face appeared, pressed against the glass. She waved with one wingtip for him to come outside.

"Greetings, Babybat," he said from the doorway. "Where is yours's mummy?"

She motioned into the distance. Megabat could just make out the silhouette of a large bat. "Is hers gone hunting?"

Babybat nodded.

"Mine was just reading a most adventuresome story. Would yours like to read togethers?"

But Babybat didn't seem interested in books. She loop-de-looped dangerously around some trees and came skidding in for a landing on the porch.

"Yours wants to fly swoopily through the dark forest?" Megabat asked.

She tugged on his wing.

"And yours wants mine to coming alsowise?"

She grinned.

An owl hooted. The tree branches shifted in the wind. Somewhere on the lake, a loon gave an eerie call that made Megabat shiver.

"Perhapsing another time. Mine gots a muchly funner idea," he said. "Coming this way."

Megabat flew past the cabins and the dining hall.

"This is being the craft room," he said, as he landed on a table with Babybat close behind. She sniffed some supplies: paint, glitter-glue, Scotch tape. Suddenly, she reared up, flared her wings, pounced on a pipe cleaner and tore at it with her fangs.

"No, no, Babybat." Megabat pulled it from her mouth. "That's not being a critterpillar. Yours can't eating that."

Babybat stuck out her bottom lip in a pout—but soon she spotted a jar of bright beads. She flew across the room.

"Stopping that, Babybat!" Megabat hollered, but it was too late. She'd buried her face in the jar and was tossing beads up in the air one by one, batting them

with her wingtip. One pinged against the light fixture and a few more bounced off the window.

Megabat glowered at her. He pointed to a box filled with pom-poms. "Playing with these while yours waits," he ordered. She couldn't hurt herself or break anything in there. "Mine will be right back with some sumplies."

Megabat had hidden in Daniel's pocket all afternoon, watching through the buttonhole. He knew what they needed for the craft he had in mind, and he made quick work of flying around the camp, gathering the things and dragging them back.

By then, Babybat had abandoned the

pom-poms and was eyeing the scissors dangerously, but Megabat distracted her just in time.

"Mine knows a wild bat like yours-self leads an adventuresome life of thrillingness," Megabat said, "so yours will loving this craft. It's being called tie . . ." He paused for dramatic effect. "And *die.*"

Babybat gasped, then grinned with all her fangs.

8

THE PRANKS

The next morning at breakfast, Cook Martina looked especially cheerful in her tall chef's hat, which, instead of its usual white, was a swirl of rainbow colors. The counselors looked joyous too. Well, their shirts did, even if their faces didn't.

"All right," Fiona said from the front of the dining hall. "Very funny. Which one of you snuck away from the fire last night and tie-dyed the staff uniforms?"

Nobody would admit to it. Vijay eyed his campers suspiciously. "You know," he said, "if you prank the counselors, we'll get you back."

Daniel slipped a strawberry to Megabat, who was hiding under his napkin. "Are you *sure* you don't know anything about this?" he whispered.

"Mine was explorationing caves," Megabat said innocently. He mashed the berry in his mouth while crossing his blue- and purple-tinged wingtips behind his back to cancel out the lie. After all, it wasn't *his* fault. How could he have known that the white laundry he'd borrowed belonged to the grown-ups

or that Babybat would be so enthusiastic
about arts and crafts?

It was camp Olympics day. So right after
breakfast, the kids took part in a
beanbag toss, three-legged race and
egg-on-a-spoon challenge. Megabat was
boiling hot inside Daniel's pocket, and
the campers were all sweating in the sun.
Everyone was relieved—at first—when
Vijay brought out paper cups and a big
pitcher of icy-cold orange drink.

"Mmmmmmm. Juice of the orange!
This will be most roofreshing," Megabat
said. Daniel offered him the straw,
only—"Pah! Dust-gusting!" No sooner

had he sipped it than he was spitting the
liquid all over Daniel's shirt, and he
wasn't the only one who didn't like it.

"Ugh. That's NOT orangeade," a girl
in a red shirt yelled.

"Gross!" a boy with a baseball cap

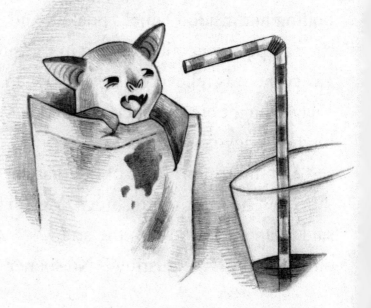

whimpered. "Ew. Get it out of my mouth!"

"What *IS* this?"

Daniel and the other boys from Cabin 8 were spitting onto the grass when they heard the sound of laughter. The counselors were doubled over, gasping for air—especially Vijay. "Gotcha!" he said with a huge smile. "We switched the orange drink mix with cheese powder."

"If you guys could see your faces right now," Fiona cackled.

"Okay, now it's *on*!" Irwin announced later that afternoon. It was raining, and the kids were gathered in the games room doing puzzles and playing board games. "I can still taste that cheese juice."

So could Megabat. Inside Daniel's pocket, he was sucking on a grape from lunch, but it wasn't helping much.

"We've got to think of something epic to get them back," Gus agreed as he threw the dice and moved his piece up a ladder in the game he was playing.

"We could put plastic wrap over the toilet seats?" a girl named Tammy suggested.

"Nah. Too messy," Rusty pointed out. "Plus, what if a camper needs to go?"

"My dad put underpants up the flagpole when he went here," Daniel offered, as he worked away at a puzzle.

"A classic," Irwin conceded, "but we need something even bigger."

By campfire-time, the kids were no closer to deciding on a prank to pull, and Megabat was so preoccupied worrying about the scary forest and haunted bat cave that he didn't help much.

"Has yours ever done a jigsaw puzzle?" he asked when Babybat showed up again that night and tried to tug him into the spooky woods. "Mine knows of a most dangerous one."

That got her attention.

He took her to the games room and held up the box. "It's being a crunchodile!"

Babybat examined the sharp-toothed, bumpy-skinned animal in the picture. She even helped sort edge pieces for a while, but she must have grown bored and decided to go exploring because— just as Megabat was fitting together pieces to make a ghastly, glassy crunchodile eye—

CRASH!

Boxes of puzzles began flying off the shelves.

"Babybat!" he yelled. But she was too busy lying in the giant pile of mixed-up pieces, flapping her wings, to answer.

"Not cool, guys!" Vijay said at breakfast the next morning. "Harmless pranks are one thing, but whoever dumped out twenty-five one-thousand-piece puzzles in the games room last night went too far. We'll never be able to sort them out!"

"Was that you guys?" One of the girls from Cabin 12 was leaning across the breakfast table.

"Nope," Irwin answered. "You?"

Nobody seemed to know who was responsible—except, of course, for Megabat—but he wasn't about to get himself or Babybat in trouble.

Thankfully, he had an idea for a nice quiet activity for that night that couldn't possibly go wrong.

"Ours will be crafting fun and fancy friendship bracelets!" he announced when Babybat showed up to take him exploring. She whined and motioned to the forest with her head, but Megabat held firm. He'd watched kids make bracelets at the picnic tables that day during free time. It looked easy—not to mention safe!

"Yours will be loving it," he promised. "Seeing all the colorful strings?"

Babybat *did* admire the bright shades Megabat had gathered. They found a picnic table and set to work.

"Firsting of all, ours must choosing colors."

Babybat liked red, blue and purple.

"Next, ours must measuring the strings." Using their mouths, they unwound the colors and stretched them out. "Stopping! That's being enough!" But Babybat had already unwound her spools right to the ends and moved on to the next step. "Undoubtedly, yours must tying knots now," Megabat said, "but not quites like that!"

Babybat's strings weren't going neatly one under the other to form tidy rows. Instead, she was flying every which way, hooking them on branches, tangling them around rocks and stringing them between buildings like party decorations.

Megabat buried his head in his wings and sighed.

He did have to admit it looked pretty though . . . especially in the morning light the next day when the counselors found it.

"Very funny, guys!" Vijay said to the campers, who were admiring the decorations and were every bit as puzzled as the counselors were. "Now clean it up."

It was hard work untangling the strings—especially in the high places— and by the time they were done that and the day's activities of sailing, orienteering and basket weaving, everyone was tired . . . especially Megabat. Keeping up with camp fun plus his nights with Babybat was wearing him out. In fact, he didn't have the energy to come up with a better plan when Babybat showed up wanting to go flying again.

"Perhapsing ours could be playing naptime." He flopped down on the bunk he shared with Daniel.

Tut-tut-tut. Eeeeek. Eeeeeek.

Babybat motioned out the window as she nattered at him.

"Or hide-and-goes-seeks. Mine will be hiding first." He pulled a corner of Daniel's sleeping bag over his head and closed his eyes, but Babybat tugged it off with her teeth and screeched at him.

It was clear that her patience was used up. They'd done what Megabat wanted to do three nights in a row. Now it was her turn to choose. And her choice was the scary forest and the deep, dark cave.

"Mine's too nappy for flying tonight," he told her, finally. "Going by yoursself."

First Babybat pouted. Then she threw a tiny tantrum complete with hissing and snarling. But eventually she left, letting the door slam behind her. Megabat yawned and closed his eyes. He was nearly asleep, in fact, when the voices on the front porch roused him.

"I can't wait to see the looks on their faces when they brush their teeth tonight."

Megabat flapped up to the window and spied out. It was Vijay and Fiona.

Vijay was holding a big box that said
SALT on it.

"The old salty toothbrush prank never
hurt anyone," she said. "And they've got

it coming after all the pranks they've pulled this week. Although, I've got to admit, seeing Cook Martina in that rainbow hat every day is pretty funny."

"Hey! Shhhh!" Vijay said. "Did you hear that?"

"Hear what?" Fiona asked.

"That rustling. I think it's coming from my cabin roof. I've been hearing scratching up there all week. Especially in the mornings. And look!" Vijay pointed to the narrow gap in the cabin's peaked roof.

"A bat!"

Both counselors ducked as Babybat squeezed out of the gap, streaked across the sky and disappeared into the forest.

"Uh-oh," Fiona said. "Where there's one roosting, there are usually more. We'd better tell the custodian to set a trap."

Megabat gasped. A trap!

"I'll check if he can come do it right away while the kids are still at the campfire," Vijay said.

Megabat hung in a shadowy corner while the two counselors came in and gleefully salted the kids' toothbrushes, but as soon as they'd gone, he flew down.

"Mine must saving the day," he said to himself. "Before Babybat and Batzilla fallings into the trap."

Except, before he'd taken a single step toward the door, he realized the trouble with that plan. To warn Babybat and Batzilla, he'd have to go through the deep, dark forest to the haunted cave— and he'd have to do it all alone!

9

THE FEARSOME FOREST

Passing through the spooky forest was going to be tricky, but there had to be a way.

"What would Diamond Foot be doing?" Megabat asked himself.

It was easy enough to find out. He flapped up to Irwin's bunk and opened the book. There was his hero, boldly battling the five-headed lizard with bad breath . . . but, what was that on his face?

"Aha!" Megabat said. "His is wearing a mask!" Megabat searched Daniel's suitcase, hoping he'd packed one, but no. He'd have to improvise. He gnawed two

eye holes in a tube sock and pulled it over his head.

"What's else? Aha! His is having tools."

Diamond Foot didn't always rely on just his mighty, glittering foot. He also had a ray gun that went *pshew-pshew* and shot sonic stun beams at the lizard. Megabat looked high and low, but there wasn't a single sonic stun gun in Cabin 8.

"Aha!" There *was* a grape juice box in the special care package Talia, Birdgirl and Priscilla had given them. If he stuck the straw in, he could squeeze it at enemies. "Standing back." He wrapped his wings around the juice box and practiced his tough-bat act. "Or mine will juice yours. And juice of the grape makings big, bad stains!" He knew because he'd spilled it on the couch once. Daniel's mother had *not* been happy.

Now he was ready. Only . . . Megabat paused near the door. He still didn't feel brave. Something must be missing.

He went back to study the book and smacked himself in the forehead. It was obvious! Sparkle lines were emanating from Diamond Foot's magnificent boot. He was aglow with bravery. Well, Megabat could glow too.

He decorated his wings with the glow-in-the-dark eyeball stickers from the care package, then, by the light of the full moon, he balanced the juice box on his

back and took off into the shadowy
woods.

"Mine's coming, Babybat!" he
proclaimed. He flapped his wings with
all his might, but the heavy juice box
made it hard to fly straight.

"Mine will warn yours of the evil plot
to trap the batses!"

It was also difficult to see out the holes in the sock. He veered around a big evergreen, just managing to miss the trunk.

"Mine will saving yours and Batzilla from capturization!"

He plummeted low, almost to the ground under the weight of the juice box, then flapped harder than ever trying to get some lift.

"Mine will be so muchly brave that—AH!" Megabat cried.

Something had grabbed him! He reached for his juice box to spray his way free but, as he twisted, it rolled off his back and fell to the forest floor with a thud. Still the grabby beast clutched him, yanking the sock mask right off his head.

"Ahhhhhhhh!" Megabat screamed when he found himself falling. "Oof." He landed in a bed of pine needles and checked himself all over. He seemed to be all okay.

Only . . . "Wh-wh-what's is that being?"

Straight ahead, there was the snapping of twigs. A shadow moved in the darkness.

He looked right: more shadows.

He looked left: shadows, shadows and more shadows!

They surrounded him, circling.

"Helping MINE!" Megabat hollered.

"PEEEEEEEEZE! Helping mine!"

He wrapped his wings around himself and rocked back and forth. Long minutes seemed to pass, although they might have been only seconds.

"Megabat? Is that you?"

He blinked into the beam of a flashlight and saw the gleam of silvery braces. Irwin! And, right behind him, Daniel!

Megabat swooped toward his friend and buried his face in Daniel's sweatshirt. "Mine was so ascared."

"It's okay." Daniel stroked his fur. "I'm here now. We were on our way back to the cabin to get a drink of water and we heard you call for help. What happened?"

It took a moment for Megabat to calm

down enough to explain. "There was being a terrible grabby beast," he said, taking shuddery breaths. "It did pull mine's sock mask away! Mine's juice box ray gun did fall. And m-m-m-most spooky shadowy creatures circled arounds and arounds."

Irwin shone his flashlight in a wide arc. "You mean, these shadowy creatures?" Megabat unglued his face from Daniel's shirt to look. Crouched in the darkness was a family of bunny rabbits. They froze in the beam of light. Their eyes flashed red, then they turned tail and hopped away.

Irwin laughed. "I think you landed in a rabbit den."

Just bunnies?

"And maybe this was the grabby beast?" Daniel suggested. He unhooked the tube sock from a tree branch where it was snagged.

Just a branch?

"What were you doing out here all alone, anyway?" Daniel asked. "Where's Babybat?"

"Hers flyinged to the caves to find hers's mummy," Megabat explained.

He told all about the bat trap the custodian was going to set.

"Megabat knew mine had to warning theirs!" he proclaimed. Then he added sadly, "Only mine was too afeared."

"But . . . you've been exploring the

forest and caves every night since we got here," Daniel pointed out.

Megabat had to admit that he hadn't been. Not even once. And then he had to tell Daniel and Irwin who'd *really* played the pranks—and how they'd all begun because Megabat was avoiding the spooky woods and creepy cave and trying to keep Babybat busy in safer places.

"Only theys wasn't pranks!" he said in his defense. "Babybat is just most busy and getsings into everythings!"

"Gee." Daniel grinned. He peeled a glow-in-the-dark eyeball sticker off Megabat's wing. "I wonder what it's like to have a friend like *that*?"

Megabat held up his wings to show
the remaining stickers. He motioned to
the chewed tube sock that Daniel had

stuffed in his pocket, then the grape juice box that had fallen to the ground. "Mine prepared mineself in all the outfittings of bravery. But it was none use. Mine's just a fraidy-bat." He hung his head in shame. "A scaredy, little fraidy-bat."

"No, you're not, Megabat," Irwin said kindly, but Megabat didn't believe him.

"Yours can jumping off the dock and climbing to the tippiest top of the ropes course," Megabat pointed out. "Yours knows nonething about fraidy-bats."

It was Daniel who managed to make Megabat feel a little better by telling the truth. "Okay. So maybe you *are* a little bit of a fraidy-bat. But so what? What's wrong with that?"

"Fraidy-bats isn't brave like Diamond Foot," Megabat pointed out. "Or twinkle-toothed and fear-free like Irwin."

"I wish!" Irwin said. "Braces don't make you brave. And neither do costumes or ray guns." He picked up the juice box. "Plus, nobody in real life is like Diamond Foot. *'A brilliant hero has zero fear-o.'*" He scoffed at Diamond Foot's catchphrase. "Sounds cool, but seriously? Everyone's afraid of something."

"Even yours?" Megabat asked.

"Um. Yeah," Irwin said, like it was obvious. "For example, I'd never have had the guts to lick a caterpillar." He grimaced. "Also, just so you know, I only

started doing cannonballs last year . . .
and that's the highest I've ever been on
the ropes course. I was scared the first
time I came here too, but this is my third
year. And I'm sorry I laughed at you just
now. If I didn't have my flashlight, I'd
have been freaked out by those bunny
rabbits too."

Just then, there was a snapping of
twigs. Both the boys and the bat jumped,
then Irwin redirected his flashlight.

"See?" He'd illuminated a deer in
a thicket of trees. It nodded its graceful
head, as if to say hello, then bounded off
into the night. "Once you shine a light
on scary stuff and kind of get to know
it, it's usually not so bad anymore."

"Huh." Megabat watched the deer's spotted bum leap away. He was starting to understand. "Nicely to meet yours, deer!" he called out.

After all, getting to know things had worked for Daniel. Daniel had been scared of Lake PieCrust, but only until he dipped his toes in and saw there were no leeches. And he'd been worried about the camp food, but only until he'd tasted the garlic bread. In fact, even bugs had started to seem a little bit interesting to Daniel once he'd met Whiffy.

The only problem was . . . the idea of taking those first few steps into the dark woods was making Megabat's tummy do flips and flops.

"Will yourses coming with mine?" Megabat asked Daniel and Irwin. "To helping warn Babybat and Batzilla?"

"Of course!" Daniel said. "Doing stuff together always makes it easier."

"Not to mention safer," Irwin said. "You really shouldn't walk alone in the woods, especially at night."

So they set off together.

As they made their way down the path, Megabat rode on Daniel's shoulder and Irwin shone the light up ahead.

"Ah!" Daniel almost tripped where the ground was uneven. "What was that? A snake?!"

Megabat clutched tightly to his friend's shirt, but when Irwin pointed the light down they could see it clearly.

Just a big tree root!

"Nicely to meet yours, tree root!" Megabat said, and he felt his fear dissolve a little.

On they went. They spotted some moths, a flying squirrel and a ring-eyed raccoon. "Nicely to meet yours, foresty friends!" Megabat called into the darkness.

The terrain got rockier and a little steeper. "We're almost at the edge of the campgrounds now," Irwin said. "It's where we'll find the cave."

And not a minute later—

"Ummm . . . Wow," Daniel said in a shaky voice.

It was easy to see how Devil's Mouth got its name. The yawning opening of the cave looked monstrous in the darkness.

"You know," Irwin said, "maybe we

shouldn't go in after all. We can always come back and warn the bats tomorrow . . . maybe in the daylight."

But Megabat knew it would be too late by sunrise. If Babybat and Batzilla returned to their roost at the cabin, they'd surely be captured. And yes, this cave was MUCH scarier than bunny rabbits, a deer, a tree root, some moths, a flying squirrel and a raccoon combined . . . but now that Megabat had said hello to all those things, perhaps he was just brave enough.

"Waiting here." Megabat's wings shook as he flew toward the mouth of the cave. He stopped at the edge. For a moment, he thought of turning back, but then, gathering all his courage, "Hello?" he said, ever so softly. "Nicely to meet yours."

An answer came from inside the cave. *"Hello? . . . Nicely to meet yours."*

Megabat jumped back. Was it a ghost? Perhaps. But, if so, it was quite polite. "Huh!?" he said.

"Huh!?" the ghost answered. It sounded just as uncertain about him as he felt about it.

"Mine won't hurting yours," Megabat said, a little louder.

"Mine won't hurting yours. Mine won't hurting yours," the voice answered.

"Daniel. Irwin. Coming here. The cave ghost is being most friendly!"

Irwin approached with the flashlight. Megabat could see the gleam of his braces as he smiled. "That's not a ghost, it's an echo," he explained. "See? Echo! Echo!" he yelled into the cave.

"*Echo! Echo!*" the cave called back.

Suddenly, a high-pitched screech filled the night. Both boys jumped back. Only Megabat wasn't scared. He recognized the shrill song. In fact, it was so ear-splittingly awful that he'd know it anywhere.

"Babybat!" he called, and he launched himself into the cave.

As his eyes adjusted to the darkness, Megabat flew in circles, taking it all in. A little stream burbled along the ground

and the walls shimmered with bits of crystal. What's more, a whole colony of bats was swooping around joyfully, playing what looked like a big game of tag.

"They're catching bugs," said Daniel, who'd followed Megabat inside.

"Mosquitoes, to be exact," Irwin added, swatting one on his arm. "The worst kind of bugs. *That's* why we hardly ever get bitten at camp!"

Was this the place Megabat had been so worried about? It was wondrous! Magical! The best, best fun! He went deeper into the cave and a few wild bats held out their wingtips for high fives as he passed.

"Babybat!"

"Babybat! Babybat! Babybat!"

He swooped through the echoes and around the shimmery bits of rock that hung from the cave's roof.

"Where is yours?"

"Where is yours? Where is yours? Where is yours?"

Aha! There she was up ahead, singing her dreadful song.

"Mine's gots to warn yours," he called out. But he knew there was no real rush now. He could tell her in a little while.

Her eyes lit up as she swooped gleefully toward him, overjoyed that he'd finally come out to play.

10

THE FINAL PRANK

It was Daniel who came up with the ultimate prank on the counselors.

They planned it for the very last campfire of the week. Megabat wriggled in anticipation all through the singing of the silly songs, but finally, it was time.

"Okay, guys," Fiona said. "Get ready for the last ghost story of the week. It's the scariest one yet."

Irwin raised his hand. "Actually, if the counselors don't mind, Cabin 8 wants to tell a story tonight."

Fiona looked to Vijay, who glanced at the other counselors. They all shrugged. "Fine with us," Vijay said.

Daniel stood up. He looked around the circle at the gathered kids and counselors, then, even though his voice shook a little at first, he spoke loud and clear. "This is a true story," he said. "In fact . . ." He paused ominously. "It's happening at this very campfire . . . tonight."

That got the counselors' attention.

"Rumor has it there are some counselors here," Daniel went on, "who once tried to trap bats."

Vijay and Fiona exchanged a nervous, puzzled glance.

"And when the bats of Camp Wildwood heard about it, well, they weren't too happy. So they started to beat their wings."

The twins stood up. They waved their arms slowly for an especially spooky effect. "*FLAP. FLAP. FLAP,*" they said together.

"Real cute, guys," Fiona said.

"*FLAP. FLAP. FLAP.*" The twins said it louder this time.

"You're gonna have to try harder than that if you want to scare us," Vijay added.

"In fact," Daniel went on, "the bats

were *so* angry that they decided to fly out to the campfire."

Irwin stood up and shone his flashlight around. There was nothing . . . just trees and shadows. At first the counselors looked smug, but the second Irwin switched off the flashlight, a tall counselor from Cabin 4 jumped so suddenly that the marshmallow he'd been roasting fell into the fire.

Vijay followed his gaze. "AHHHHHH!" he screamed. Eerie eyeballs were glowing in the darkness all around them. A bunch of the other kids, who'd been warned that the story was a practical joke, started laughing.

The kids from Cabin 8 had used up the entire pack of stickers from Daniel and Megabat's care package. They'd stuck them to the trees earlier in the evening. The stickers had gone unnoticed before. But thanks to the light from

Irwin's flashlight, they were shining bright.

Daniel continued. "Like I was saying, the bats came to the campfire, flapping their powerful wings."

Right on cue, there was a terrific noise up above.

Megabat glanced up just in time to see Babybat leading the way as the bat colony from the cave flew overhead. All together, their wings made such a strong breeze that the fire's flames flickered. This time a few kids screamed too, and Fiona threw her hands up over her head and ducked. "What the heck?!"

"And then . . . ," Daniel continued, "one of them spoke in a thundering voice."

Irwin turned on his flashlight again. That was when Batzilla landed in front of its beam. She was huge to begin with, but thanks to the way the flashlight magnified her, her shadow loomed as tall as the trees.

Daniel nodded at Megabat. Here was his big moment! He took off into the treetops, chose a perch where he was virtually unspottable, and used his loudest, spookiest voice.

"Mine is Batzill . . . aaaaaaaah! BATZILL-AHHHHHHHHH!" he cried. "And mine is here to tell yourses that batses are friendses!"

"Okay, enough guys!" Vijay said. "Where's that voice coming from?"

"SHUSHING!" Megabat shouted. "Be listening to Batzilla!"

Vijay's mouth dropped open, but he stopped talking.

"Batses are friendses," Megabat repeated. "So do not be trapping batses or chasing thems away. For fact, batses are an important part of the egosystem."

"*Eco*system," Daniel corrected in a loud whisper, but Megabat was on a roll.

"Theys is eating pesty bugses. Suchly as munkskitos and critterpillars."

Megabat made a face. Personally, he'd never understand the appeal.

"Mine is Batzill . . . ahhhhhhhh!" he yelled. "BATZILLA!"

At that, the real Batzilla flapped her huge wings once, twice, and took off into the night sky. For a moment, there was silence except for a few of the counselors, who were clutching each other tight and breathing heavily. A bunch of girls from Cabin 3 began to roar with laughter.

"If you could see your faces right now," one of them said.

"Very funny. Okay, guys," Fiona said after she'd caught her breath. "That was pretty good."

"Seriously. How'd you do it?" Vijay asked.

"Do what?" Daniel shrugged.

"It wasn't us," Gus added.

"Yeah. It was Batzilla and her friends," Rusty finished.

"Right," Vijay said with a small smile, but his voice was a little warbly. "Nice try. Super-creative. But you didn't actually scare us. Not one bit."

Only, the very next morning, the campers were awoken by hammering.

Megabat opened his eyes groggily.

"What's going on?" Irwin said.

"I don't know," Gus answered. "But whatever it is, it's annoying."

The four boys and one bat made their way to the porch. There, in the clearing between the cabins, the counselors were hard at work building something that looked like a big birdhouse.

"It's a bat box," Vijay explained as the other counselors hoisted it up on a long pole. "We can't let bats roost in our cabins . . . but up to one hundred bats can live in one of these. Not that we believe in Batzilla," he said quickly. "But she made some pretty decent points about the ecosystem, and we

174

all hate mosquitoes, so . . ."

The rest of the morning passed
quickly, between eating a last waffle

breakfast, packing their things and saying goodbye to their new friends.

"Hurry up, guys," Vijay said. "The bus'll be here any minute."

Daniel already had his bag over one shoulder, but Megabat was still sitting in the corner. "What's wrong?" Daniel asked. "Aren't you excited to see Birdgirl, Priscilla and Talia again?"

"Undoubtedly," Megabat said sadly. "Ours didn't even have time to writes thems letters! Mine muchly wants to go home. But now it's being daylight, and mine forgotted say farewells to Babybat."

"It's okay," Daniel said. "I have an idea for how you can use the stamps from the care package when we get home."

He looked out the window and laughed, "Plus, I think Babybat said farewell to you. Come see."

Megabat flew into Daniel's pocket and they went out together. There, pulling into the clearing, was the school bus . . . but it wasn't just yellow anymore. It was wrapped in a criss-cross of colorful strings. They draped across the windows and dangled from the stop sign.

"I parked it in the lot last night," the driver said to Vijay as he got out. "I don't know what happened."

Megabat grinned. "Babybat maked mine the biggest, bussiest friendship bracelet ever!"

The driver had to clear off some of

the string before the kids could load their luggage and climb aboard, but when it was Daniel's turn to board, the driver stopped him. "Well," he said, "I'm waiting for my report. Did you have enough fun to earn this?" He tapped the Ewok's bobblehead.

"I actually had a lot more than ten kinds of fun," Daniel answered. But he and Megabat had already decided what to do—difficult as it was for Megabat, who really did love that bobblehead. "Keep it though," Daniel went on. "You can give it to the next kid who's scared to go to camp. Because I already know I'm coming back next year."

The bus driver tipped his cap. Then

Daniel and Megabat joined the busload of stinky, sleepy, sun-kissed campers headed home from the adventure of a livingtime.

To: Babybat
Batbox
Camp Wildwood
375 Green Acre Road

Dear Babybat,

Thanking yours for the bussy bracelet and a most splendiferous adventuresome time. Seeing yours next summer!

Love, Megabat

PS Mine axingdentally forgotted whiffy on the porch. Peeze be releasing him into the wild. Hiz is alsowise a most important part of the egozystem.

PPS Do not eet him, or yours will get a most stinkee sumprise.

A Little Bit about Bats

Megabat is based on a real kind of fruit bat
(or megabat) called the lesser short-nosed fruit
bat. These bats are tiny, weighing between 21 and
32 grams—which is about as heavy as an AA battery,
or a mouse—and live in South and Southeast Asia
and Indonesia (Borneo), usually in rainforests, near
gardens, near vegetation or on beaches.

Of course, even though Megabat is based on
a real kind of bat, he's also made up. I don't need to
tell you that actual bats can't talk . . . not even in the
funny way that Megabat talks! But it might be worth
mentioning that bats don't make good pets, either.

Bats are amazing creatures and an important part of our ecosystem. North-American bats eat insects, and they're rarely dangerous to humans. So if you see a bat in the wild it's okay to observe it from a distance, but don't try to touch it or trap it!

The bat boxes that Fiona and Vijay put up are real—many people put bat boxes on their property, and they really do hold hundreds of bats! Bats keep mosquitoes and other pests away, and having a bat box gives bats a safe place to roost—instead of attics, barns and camp cabin ceilings!

Acknowledgments

Putting your heart on the page (even in the form of a talking fruit bat) can be a scary thing, but having great people in your corner makes all the difference. First off, thanks to the writers I've been lucky enough to connect with through the Canadian kid-lit community, including the members of TorKidLit and my Kitchener-Waterloo area writers' group. Children's writers cheer each other on like no one I've ever met before, and it helps us all to keep writing bravely in a business that can sometimes be as nerve-racking as it is richly rewarding.

Thanks also to the great folks at Tundra Books,

where I know that Megabat and I are always in safe hands. These include Sam Swenson, Sam Devotta and many others who help to edit, design, promote and distribute Megabat. As always thank you also to my agent, the wonderful Amy Tompkins, and to Kass Reich who brings the story to life with her drawings in all the most adorable ways.

And of course, gratitude to my kids for putting up with a mom who's always talking bat . . . and to my husband for enduring the camp pranks I tested out on him for this book. (Sorry-not-sorry about the soft-serve ice cream that was actually mayo with sprinkles and chocolate sauce.) Brent, Grace and Elliot, mine loves yours bigly forevers and evers and muchly mores evers.

ANNA HUMPHREY has worked in marketing for a poetry organization, in communications for the Girl Guides of Canada, as an editor for a webzine, as an intern at a decorating magazine and for the government. None of those was quite right, so she started her own freelance writing and editing business on top of writing for kids and teens. She lives in a big, old brick house in Kitchener, Ontario, with her husband and two kids and no bats. Yet.

KASS REICH was born in Montreal, Quebec. She works as an artist and educator and has spent the majority of the last decade traveling and living abroad. She now finds herself back in Canada, but this time in Toronto. Kass loves illustrating books for all ages, like *Carson Crosses Canada*, *Sergeant Billy* and *Hamsters Holding Hands*.